TEEN
HOT LINE

DROPPING OUT OF SCHOOL

Debra Goldentyer

RSVP
RAINTREE STECK-VAUGHN
PUBLISHERS
The Steck-Vaughn Company
Austin, Texas

Consultants:
Lori Myrick Creighton, Counselor; Liberty Middle School, Madison, AL
Regina E. Manley, Counselor; Highland Park High School, Highland Park, IL
Cynthia S. Swiecki, Social Worker; Family Service Association of Bucks County, PA

Developed for Steck-Vaughn Company by Visual Education Corporation, Princeton, New Jersey
Project Director: Jewel Moulthrop
Editors: Dale Anderson, Paula McGuire
Editorial Assistant: Carol Ciaston
Photo Research: Cindy Cappa

Raintree Steck-Vaughn Publishers staff
Editor: Gina Kulch
Project Manager: Joyce Spicer
Electronic Production: Scott Melcer
Photo Editor: Margie Foster

Library of Congress Cataloging-in-Publication Data
Goldentyer, Debra, 1960-
Dropping out of school / Debra Goldentyer.
p. cm. — (Teen hot line)
Includes index.
Summary: Discusses problems teenagers face after dropping out of school and alternatives available such as night school and the GED test.
ISBN:0-8114-3526-1
1. Dropouts — United States — Juvenile literature. 2. Dropouts — United States — Attitudes — Juvenile literature. 3. Dropouts — United States — Social conditions — Juvenile literature. I. Title. II. Series.
LC143.G65 1994
371.2'913'0973—dc20 93-14251
CIP AC

Photo Credits: Cover: HMS Images/The Image Bank; **17:** Leslye Borden/PhotoEdit; **20:** © Peter Menzel/Stock Boston; **24:** Spencer Grant/Photo Researchers, Inc.; **26:** Howard Dratch/The Picture Cube; **34:** Steve Takatsuno/The Picture Cube; **39:** © Jeffry Dunn/Stock Boston; **42:** Robert Brenner/PhotoEdit; **47:** © Bob Daemmrich/Stock Boston; **52:** Rafael Macia/PhotoEdit; **55:** © Hazel Hankin/Stock Boston; **64:** Day Williams/Photo Researchers, Inc.; **72:** Bob Kramer/The Picture Cube

Printed and bound in the United States

1 2 3 4 5 6 7 8 9 0 LB 99 98 97 96 95 94

CONTENTS

What the Teen Hot Line Is All About

This book is like a telephone hot line. It answers questions about school and dropping out that may puzzle you. Answering them requires us to give you the facts. You can use those facts to make your own decisions about whether or not to finish school. So think of us as the voice on the phone, always there to answer your questions, even the hard ones.

Just so you know where we stand, here is a list of steps that we think a person should take before deciding whether to drop out of school. They focus on using common sense and finding out facts. They assume that you want to make your own decision and that you want to behave responsibly.

1. Think about the advantages you receive from high school. Don't stop at the academics; think about the social aspects of school and any benefits you might gain from extracurricular activities.

2 Think about what you might want to do for a living. Talk with career counselors or others about how much education you will need for the jobs that interest you. Find out what jobs would be open to you without a high school diploma.

3 If you're having trouble at school, try to get help from your teacher, from counselors, or from tutors.

4 If troubles at home are making it difficult for you to stay in school, think about what you can do to work out those troubles. Be sure to ask for help from a responsible adult if you need it.

5 Decide whether or not you want to finish school.

6 If you decide to stay in school, make a commitment to do the best you can and get the best grades you can. Make a commitment to get involved in some extracurricular activities, too, if they won't interfere too much with your schoolwork.

7 If you decide to leave school, be sure you have a plan before you go. Find a job or a training program that will meet your needs now or prepare you for the future.

After you read this book, we hope you will have some answers to your questions—and perhaps to some questions you hadn't thought of yet. In the back of the book is a list of sources for further information. Thinking about the issues raised in this book is an important step toward taking control of your life.

Interview

Mary Beth is 29 years old. When she was 16, she became pregnant and dropped out of tenth grade. Thirteen years later, after having had one too many dead-end jobs, she took some classes and got her high school equivalency diploma.

My father's an alcoholic. We were always scraping to make ends meet. My dad only worked off and on so my mom had to work three jobs. After she started working those three jobs, us kids weren't supervised. My father would mostly be in the bar. Starting at about the age of 13, I basically did what I wanted to do. At school, I'd say I was sick and go home. Nobody was there so I could do whatever I wanted.

I started hanging with people who used drugs. I was doing speed and acid, smoking pot, doing some cocaine, and drinking. We'd get high and walk around the streets and the mall. We did a lot of stealing.

When I did go to class, I never did the homework. You know, I was there; that's about it. I was always causing trouble with the teachers.

When I got to tenth grade, I met a guy who was four years older than I was—he was 20; I was 16. I got pregnant. I went to what they called a TAP school, for Teen Age Pregnancy. You know, you could still finish school, and they'd teach you about labor and pregnancy, and then you could go back after you had your baby. But for me, the program was too easy. This place was real loose. They'd tell you not to smoke, but I'd stand out on this balcony and smoke, and nothing happened. I mean, that didn't make sense to me, so I quit. I needed something stricter. I only lasted a couple of months. And then I never went back.

When I told my mom and dad that I was pregnant, my father told me, "You'll finish school and you'll live here." My attitude was, "Forget that." You know—when you don't get along with your parents to begin with, and they start demanding that you're going to do this and this and this, you're automatically going to do the opposite. So, I just left. I went and lived with this guy who I got pregnant by. They wanted me to come back home, and they wanted me to finish school and stuff, but I was stubborn and bull-headed and said, "No."

That was hard. As I look back on it, it was something I should have never done. You know, I should have stayed home; I should have gotten support from my family and stuff. But with being very stubborn and not wanting to live with an alcoholic, you know, I just—I thought I was better off on my own.

Living with this guy was real hard. Well, at first it was OK. Then it became real bad. You know how you feel when somebody tells you that they're going to do something for you and it doesn't happen. Like, he told me he was going to marry me. But after about 5 years, I gave up on that idea. I ended up having an 11-year relationship that was physically and mentally abusive. He would beat me and tell me I was no good.

I had my son in September of '81. But without finishing school, I couldn't just walk away from his father. Because you're out there in the world all by yourself, you're scared to death. You have the idea nobody will hire you because you don't have your high school diploma or your GED, and you haven't even grown up yet.

I'd always thought about going back to school, but then, when you don't have respect for yourself—good self-esteem—you don't do things like that. Yeah, my self-esteem was real low, with getting into the drugs and being abused. I felt like I couldn't do anything right, you know. And even though you can try and try, and they make promises that things will be better and stuff, everything always falls apart. You know, it never changes.

I wasn't thinking towards the future. I didn't have any clue what it was going to hold for me. I didn't stop to think as far as ever getting a job, how I was going to support myself. I became dependent on the child's father. And he used drugs, too, so it didn't help. Then he got laid off from his job. And he was looking for work; he was on unemployment. We ended up living with his parents for two and a half years. And that didn't work.

The unemployment ran out, and once you go on welfare, you're trapped. Because if you find a job, even though that job doesn't bring you as much as welfare does, they take the welfare away. So you're better off not getting a job, you know. It was hard. It was real hard.

A few years later the kid's father walked out on his job. So I went to work in a little restaurant. I got to be able to do everything from cooking to cleaning to cashier to waiting on people. I was lucky enough to have a hard boss. He was very strict—if things weren't done the right way, he'd jump on you.

Later I got a job in a grocery store, working in the deli-bakery. When you don't go to school, you get these low-paying jobs that go nowhere. You know, if I was still there, I'd still be in the same department and not learning anything. And the other jobs that I had, it was the same way—there was no challenge; you didn't really need any brains for it, you know?

It was hard to find a job, because everybody wants a high school diploma or GED. And if you didn't have that, they'd look down on you. I only got the grocery store job because of my sister-in-law—she was already working there. I'm sorry I left school when I did. It would have been great—being able to say that you did it, that you went all the way through school.

I loved art class, because you could be creative. You know, use your imagination. I got A's in that. But as far as math and English, reading, spelling, social studies—I didn't like those. In fact, today I feel bad 'cause, for instance, with spelling, I spell words how they sound, and not the proper way. And I wish I would have stayed in school to learn.

I would love to go back and be able to do it all over again, you know? 'Cause you miss out on a lot. I missed dating different people, meeting different people, finding out about myself, going to proms. You know, you see it on TV and stuff, and you wonder what it would be like. And the friendships—I missed the friendships. After leaving school, nobody would hang around with me. And just being able to find out what's inside yourself, and what you want to do in life. I missed all of it.

My high school was having their tenth-year reunion. But it wouldn't be the same—going back there to this reunion without graduating.

About a year ago, I went through a 28-day drug rehab program. And then when I got out, I wanted to make my life better. So I decided to get my GED. After I earned it, I had a sense of accomplishment—you know, being able to finish something—feeling proud. So it was really—I don't know, there was a lot of emotions. Because you think, I could have done this a long time ago, you know? And so you get a little mad at yourself. But I don't know, I was more—I was pleased with myself that I was able to stick with it, you know, and not procrastinate on it. Because I'm real good at procrastination.

With getting this GED, I'm going to be in an on-the-job-training program in physical therapy, and so I'm going to be working with patients who had injuries. I'll do a little office work in the afternoon. So it's a very challenging job.

I had a job interview on Monday—it was real good. With having the confidence after quitting the drugs, you get more confidence as you accomplish other things afterwards. Your self-esteem rises, you know. I think I got the job.

But I have to go to school for typing, and I know I need to go to school for spelling. I really want to go. I want to learn. Because it'll make my job a lot easier. It gives you a boost that you know you have the GED, that you accomplished that. You can then move on to your next step.

It'll be a good-paying job, and it'll be a challenge. And it won't be like your everyday work like as a cashier, where there's no challenge there. After all these years of not going to school, and raising my kid and stuff, I've never had any challenge for me. So it's going to be a real good challenge for me. I'm happy with it.

You get more accomplishments staying in school. 'Cause if you drop out, it's a hard life. 'Cause you'll never have—I can't say never, but—it will be a long struggle before you get your act together.

You know, I've learned that the hard way. When I was in school, it was fun. But when you get in with that wrong crowd, and you start thinking low about yourself—you know, that you're no good, that you're not worth anything—that stuff sticks with you.

And now with being in recovery, it's neat 'cause you're able to make your own choices—you don't have to have anybody's approval. If I would have known this when I was 16, you know, life would have been totally different. But at age 16 you think you know everything. You don't want to listen to anybody. And you just have to learn everything the hard way, which I did.

BULLETIN BOARD

Dropping Out (1989)

Percentage of Americans who are high school graduates: 81%

Percentage of teens aged 14 to 17 enrolled in school: 96%

Percentage of young adults who have dropped out of school: 13%

Top five reasons teens give for dropping out of school: didn't like school; were failing in school or could not keep up with the work; could not get along with their teachers; pregnancy; felt they "didn't belong"

Life After School (1989)

Percentage of high school graduates employed full time: 72%

Percentage of high school dropouts employed full time: 47%

Average annual income of a high school graduate with a full-time job: $15,000

Average annual income of a high school dropout with a full-time job: $12,000

Percentage of people who work who are high school graduates: 84%

Percentage of prison inmates who have not completed high school: 83%

High School Dropouts by Grade, 1991

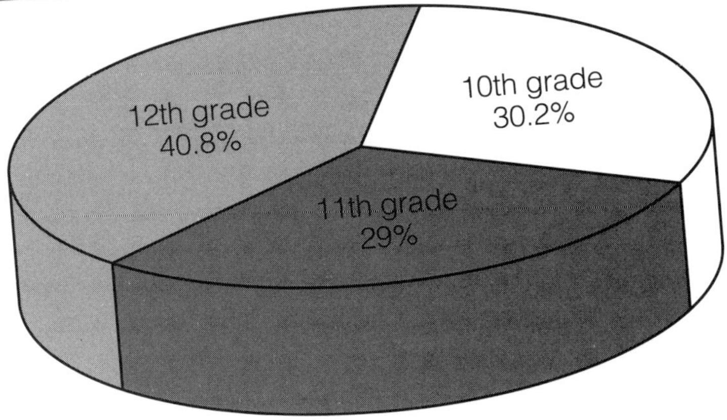

High School Dropouts by Age, 1991

Age Group	Number of Dropouts
15-16	61,000
17	97,000
18	110,000
19	44,000
20-24	35,000
Total:	347,000

Source: National Center for Education Statistics, U.S. Department of Education.

Working While in School (1989)

Percentage of high school students who work part time: 36%

Percentage of high school students who work full time: 2%

Sources: National Center for Education Statistics.

Dropout Rates in the United States: 1991.

U.S. Department of Education, 1992.

Simons, Janet M., Belva Finlay, and Alice Yang. The Adolescent and Young Adult Fact Book. Children's Defense Fund, 1991.

Snyder, Thomas D. Youth Indicators, 1991. U.S. Department of Education, 1991.

CHAPTER 1

Communicating

Q My name's Tyrone and I'm 16. I'm in a rap band. We're doing really well, and we're starting to "make it." At this point, the band has decided that school is just in the way. Even though I'm doing so well with my music, my mother won't let me quit school. How do I convince her that school isn't important?

A You already know the most important step—discussing this with your mother. Leaving school and choosing a career aren't decisions you can easily make on your own. When you talk to your mother you should be prepared to convince her that you're right. But you should also be prepared to listen to her thoughts. Do you know why she won't let you quit?

• • • • • • • • • • • •

Q Yeah, sure, she thinks it's important that I know who discovered penicillin and stuff like that. Like I care, right?

A Is that really what she thinks is the most important part of school?

• • • • • • • • • • • •

Q Well, sort of. Mom's convinced that this band is going nowhere. She doesn't understand our music. She says we'll never make any money, and we'll end up on the streets.

A And you're absolutely sure that you're really going to make it?

• • • • • • • • • • • •

Q Well, I know we're good. We've been playing for a few years. We're getting good gigs. People in the business have told me that we have the sound and the look.

A Have you told your mother that? What does she say?

• • • • • • • • • • • •

Q She says, sure some people leave school early and become rich and famous. But that's not likely to happen to me. She says people form new bands every day and our chances of making it are pretty slim. She says we'd better have something else to fall back on.

A It doesn't sound like she's trying to stop your musical career. She's just suggesting that you keep your options open.

• • • • • • • • • • • •

Q Yeah, but school is in the way. All our gigs are at night. The guys and I need the daytime to practice. If I put in as much time going to school and doing homework as she wants, I'd have to give up my music.

A But you think there may be some truth to what she says about you having something to fall back on?

Q Well, I guess it wouldn't hurt.

A Why don't you ask your mom if you and she can sit down and talk? Tell her your concerns about school getting in the way. Then listen to her. And listen with an open mind. After you talk, you might want to do some exploring—learn a little about the music business. Ask your "people in the business" how many bands are trying to make it and how many actually do.

You know your mother cares about you and wants the best for you. Maybe you and she can find a compromise. For instance, maybe you could go to school a couple of evenings a week when you weren't playing; although it might take you longer to finish. Maybe there's a program in your school that would give you practice time.

Q But it's not just my problem. The other band members are counting on me. If I don't leave school, they may just replace me with someone who will.

A That may be true. But it's your future you're planning. If you decide that your mother's right—that you need something to fall back on—you'll have to make some tough choices.

Remember, this is your decision to make, not your friends' decision. The decision you make today could affect the rest of your life. You owe it to yourself to make it carefully.

Making Your Decision

Before making your decision, gather all the facts you can. You say your band is pretty good. You've been playing for a while now, and you're starting to make some money. People are beginning to tell you that you have what you need to make it.

Starting a band takes time and dedication as well as talent. Although it will take longer to graduate, you may be able to attend school part-time while the band gets established.

But you're not stupid. What your mother says is true: A new band is formed every day. And for every band that makes it big, there are hundreds that never do. You know that it takes more than good music to make it—it takes hard work and dedication, good connections, a whole lot of lucky breaks, and time to get recognition.

So, the question is, what are your real chances of making it? What can you do to protect yourself and get where you want to be in the future?

■ First, examine the facts. Learn as much as you can about the music business. Talk to as many people as you can and get as many viewpoints as possible. Read about other musicians whom you admire. Learn from their mistakes. Did they finish school? If they didn't, do they regret their decisions? Did any ever decide to go back to school later? Why? Think about what you'd give up by leaving. You might even want to write a list of the pros and cons of leaving high school early.

■ Second, examine your feelings. Are you thinking of dropping out because you want to or because your friends want you to? Are you sure the band will make it? What if it doesn't—how would that feel? Would you miss school if you left? Is there any other career that you could pursue if the band doesn't work out? Would it require a diploma? What do you see yourself doing in five years or ten years? Will leaving school get in the way of any of these goals? What do your instincts tell you?

■ Finally, make your decision.

Communicating Your Decision

Communicating your decision can be as hard as making your decision, but it's just as important. Let's say that you decide to stay in school and get your diploma. You must tell the other band members what you've decided. Unless you tell them clearly, they may not understand that your decision is final. In that case, they may continue to put pressure on you to drop out of school. You would have to communicate your decision very clearly and very definitely.

Planning the Conversation

Peer pressure sometimes makes people say and do things they don't want to say and do. It's hard to have a meaningful conversation with friends if you are feeling pressured.

Plan in advance what you want to say. You worked hard to make your decision, and you know why you made it. Plan to share your reasons and be prepared to explain your position clearly.

Having the Conversation

Start the conversation by telling your friends how you feel. Tell them that you like and respect them, but you don't feel it makes sense for you to leave school. Tell them about the alternatives you and your mother explored. Then tell them what path you've chosen and why.

Give your friends a chance to respond, and listen to what they say. Don't argue. The purpose of your conversation is to tell them which decision you've made, not to convince them that you are right or they are wrong. Leave it to your friends to make their own decisions about what's right for them.

Of course, if you tell your friends you are staying in school, they may throw you out of the band. Since you already know that is one of the risks of your decision, be prepared to accept it. They may become angry and insistent. If so, make it clear that you've made your decision and intend to stick by it. They will have to decide what they want to do about it.

Still, your friends may surprise you. Sometimes when you communicate your feelings to friends, you find that they share many of the same feelings. If your friends aren't sure that it's wise to leave school, they may have doubts about their own decisions. They may welcome the opportunity to talk about those doubts and explore alternatives.

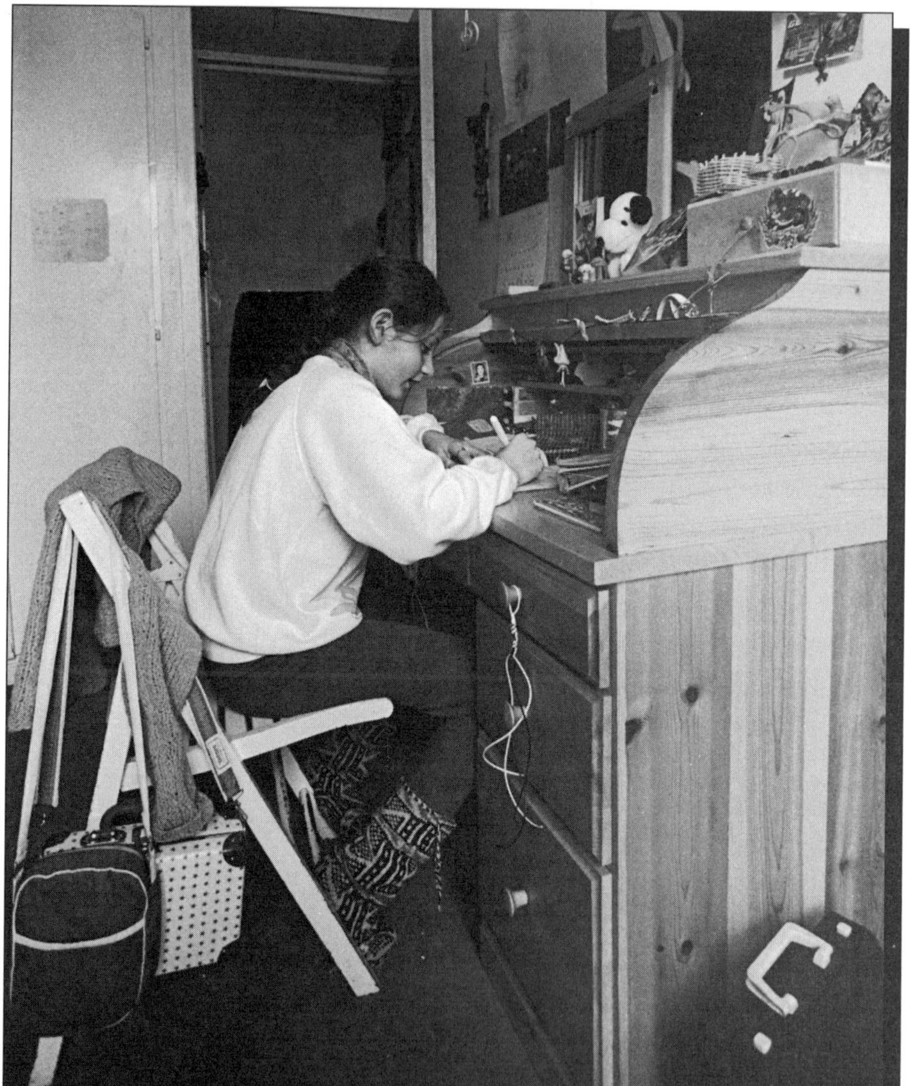

If you decide to stay in school, you should be prepared to continue with your studies seriously.

Sticking to Your Decision

Once you've made your decision and explained it clearly to your friends, there are some situations that you need to be prepared for.

■ Don't let someone talk you out of your decision. You can change your mind, but only if you decide to.

■ Commit yourself. If you decide to stay in school, don't do it halfway. Just showing up for class is not good enough. In order to graduate, you will have to devote enough time and energy to homework and studying. If you are not going to do it seriously, don't do it.

■ Don't put yourself in situations that might make it hard for you to stick to your decision. If you stay in the band, be sure your friends know when you are and aren't available. If they continue to put pressure on you to practice longer or skip school, remind them of your decision.

Learning to think through a situation rationally without allowing emotions to influence you too much can be difficult. It may force you to make some short-term sacrifices. But, once learned, it is a skill you will use for the rest of your life. It can be the difference between being a kid and becoming an adult. And that can be a source of pride and self-confidence!

CHAPTER 2

What School's For

Q My name's Kirk. I'm 17 and I work in my father's store after school. He says whenever I'm ready, he'll take me on full time. Since I have a job lined up and since I'm going to take over his business anyway, why should I bother to finish school? I mean, my dad quit school at 17, and he did pretty well.

A Your high school years are not something you should give up without careful thought. It's great that your dad did well, but just because he did well without a diploma doesn't mean that you will, too. The world has changed, and it's much harder to succeed without a high school diploma than it was in the past.

You say you're going to take over your dad's store someday. As the boss, you'll probably be in charge of setting employees' pay scales, paying taxes, and pricing the merchandise. How are your math skills? Of course, you can hire an accountant to do bookkeeping for you, but nothing can substitute for your knowing your own business.

Other academic skills may be equally important. In English class you learn writing, grammar, and vocabulary. Classes in social studies and civics teach you about business trends, history, labor unions, and economics—all extremely important matters to people who own businesses.

In difficult economic times like the ones we face today, it's best to go into your career as well prepared as possible for the challenges you'll face. That's what high school is for. The more background you have, the better you'll be able to handle your first full-time job.

All Americans are required to go to school until they reach a certain age. That age differs from state to state, but in most states, you must stay in school until you're 16. Staying in school is not only the law, but also a good idea. It may be good for you socially and mentally. It can help you prepare for your career and for the unexpected challenges in the future.

Social Life

School teaches you more than the basic subjects. It also teaches you about growing up. In fact many of the most important things you learn in high school will have little to do with the classes you take.

High school may be the last place you'll ever be where everyone is about the same age as you. Because most students are within the same age range, they are facing the same kind of personal problems you face. Most are struggling with issues of growing up—such as dating, becoming independent, dealing with others, coping with peer pressure, and making decisions about the future. Your classmates share your questions and are well acquainted with similar periods of moodiness, depression, and confusion. By spending time together in school, you can help one another work through problems.

If you go out into the business world while your peers are still in school, you'll lose that chance. You'll be confronting a whole new set of problems. You'll need to find a job, support yourself, satisfy your boss, and work long hours. In the business world, you'll be surrounded by adults, not fellow teens, so you probably won't get much support for kids' problems.

Being able to share your concerns about growing up with classmates who are dealing with the same issues is one of the advantages of staying in school.

Morris dropped out of school when he was 16. He says, "I had a good job and I thought school was just for kids. But now when I look back, I'm sorry I left. Since I wasn't around, my friends didn't include me in their parties and plans. Pretty soon, I knew very few people my age. Most of the people I hung around with were from work—they were older, married, and had kids of their own. And although it may sound silly, I wish I hadn't missed my senior prom."

The Chance to Learn

Some people find it hard to believe, but schoolwork can actually be fun. When you learn to read well or handle mathematics, you open up new worlds for yourself. You become better able to understand what's going on in the world around you. That means you'll enjoy yourself more in that world. Even subjects like history and science—which may seem remote to your life—can be valuable. They help you understand why people behave as they do and how our world came to take its current shape. You can even learn about people from the past or from another place who faced problems similar to yours. How they solved those problems may help you find your own solutions.

Learning can help you feel good about yourself, too. One of the ways that people develop a feeling of self-worth is by mastering challenges—by learning to do new things. Think of how great you felt when you first learned to ride a bike or sink a jump shot.

It's hard to feel good about yourself if you give up. But people who stick with a problem—who persevere—develop confidence in their ability to meet future challenges. Learning in school can help you master many kinds of challenges. Read the interview with Mary Beth at the beginning of the book. Notice how much better she felt after getting her GED. Why not stay in school and develop that good feeling about yourself—rather than waiting 11 years, as she did?

Preparing for Work

In school, you're required to do all sorts of homework and exercises, such as research assignments, public speaking, report writing, debates, and group projects. Certainly, one reason your teachers assign these activities is to help you learn the material in the course. But another reason is to teach you important practical skills.

Learning Skills for Life

Knowing how to study and how to write reports is essential for anyone going into business. Learning how to do research, think critically, defend your position, and speak publicly will be important throughout your career, whether you plan to be a business owner, a nurse, a salesperson, a police officer, a teacher, or nearly anything else. Writing clearly and spelling correctly are crucial skills for office workers, salespeople, police officers, and people in hundreds of other occupations.

Many workers—not just cashiers and bank tellers, but also administrative assistants and salespeople—need to have good math skills. Although most math operations are now done by electronic calculators and computers, there may not be one available when you need it.

School also teaches important lessons in discipline—lessons that will carry over into your work life. Success in school depends on showing up on time every day, alert, attentive, and ready to work. Success in the business world is based on the same sound work habits. Employers want workers who make an effort to earn their pay. Those who work hard are rewarded more than those who shirk. In fact, workers who don't show up or don't do the job often are fired.

High school teaches skills for life. Many jobs, such as supermarket checkout clerk, require workers to have good math skills.

All these skills are important, not just for getting a job in the first place, but for advancement. To earn promotions, workers must have excellent communication skills, strong math skills, good work habits, and a strong ability to work with others.

Choosing a Career

Kirk knows what he's going to do when he leaves school, but most kids don't. That's another reason why high school is valuable. It gives you a chance to learn about careers, decide which ones you may be interested in, and begin to prepare yourself for them.

Many high schools offer interesting electives such as journalism, computer technology, metalworking, business management, law, or economics. By taking some of these courses, you can explore career options and find a field that interests you.

Look at extracurricular activities, too. Most schools have drama clubs, student orchestras or bands, organized sports, a student newspaper, a yearbook, academic clubs, and a student council. Getting involved in these programs can teach you things you know little about. They're fun and enjoyable, and teens who leave school don't have the chance to participate in any of them.

An extracurricular activity may even help you choose a career. For example, when Brian signed up as the photo assistant for his school yearbook, he knew little about photography. He discovered he loved it and is now a news photographer for a national magazine. Gloria says an extracurricular activity helped her immensely. If she hadn't been in her high school play, she never would have overcome her fear of speaking in public. She's now a lawyer and speaks confidently to judges and juries all the time.

High schools also offer access to guidance counselors, who have information about careers. They know which skills will be in demand in years to come, and they can recommend

Extracurricular Activities

High Schools offer a wide variety of extracurricular activities. Here are some activities that might be available at an average high school.

Sports Teams	Football Wrestling Soccer Baseball Field Hockey	Volleyball Softball Basketball Track and Field
Boosters	Cheerleaders Color Guard	Drill Team
Arts	Band Chorus Art Club	Orchestra Drama Club Film/Video Club
Literary	School Newspaper	Literary Magazine
Academic Clubs	Foreign Language Club *(French, German, Spanish, Italian)* Science Club	Math Club Public Speaking and Debate Club National Honor Society Computer Club
Community Service	Key Club Future Business Leaders Future Teachers	Environment Club Future Nurses 4-H Club

Extracurricular activities offer students an opportunity to become involved in a field of interest, which may, in turn, help to choose a career.

careers that fit your interests and abilities. They know what type of education is required for the career you want, and they can help you develop a plan to get you where you want to go. Once you're out of high school, exploring possible careers will never again be so easy.

The New Generation

Kirk and his father might not think it's a bad idea for Kirk to leave high school, especially since Kirk's father did well even without finishing high school himself. Your parents and many of your friends' parents may be like Kirk's dad. But their success hides an important truth: A complete education was less essential in the past than it is now. There used to be many jobs that required little formal education or skills training. People who started at the lowest level stood a good chance of being promoted to better jobs if they were quick learners and worked hard. In addition, people like Kirk's father were able to open stores or start their own businesses without high school diplomas. That's not common any longer.

Life in the 1990s

Earning a living is difficult in the 1990s. Since the days when your parents began their careers, America has faced many years of recession and economic hard times. More and more companies are reducing their work forces and laying off people. There are fewer entry-level jobs and fewer opportunities to start new businesses.

Companies that are hiring can afford to be selective; they choose only the best-educated job applicants. When the competition for jobs is stiff, you need to have certain minimum qualifications before an employer will even consider you for a position. A high school diploma is one of those minimum qualifications. In fact, some career analysts think that a college education is now a minimum for most jobs.

The few jobs that remain for those without high school diplomas—such as working in fast-food restaurants, answering telephones, entering data into computers—are dead-end jobs. Like dead-end streets, they lead nowhere. These jobs offer very little room to grow—there's nothing to be promoted to. Even if someone can manage to live on them for a year or two, these jobs won't generate enough income in the future to cover such growing needs as the demands of a family.

Keep in mind, too, that many of your friends' parents may have left school to join the armed services. They came out of the military with marketable skills or with scholarships to continue their education. Today, the armed services do not accept anyone who does not have a high school diploma.

No Guarantees

Remember, there are no guarantees in life. Even if, like Kirk, you have a job lined up, that doesn't mean you'll have smooth sailing. Many businesses that did extremely well in the 1970s and 1980s—even some that have been around for generations—are suffering in the 1990s. Without careful management, Kirk's father's store may face the same fate as many others. If he wants to give the store the best chance he can, Kirk needs to be prepared. He needs to know math, marketing, management, and economics. Unless he's well educated and prepared to meet crises and challenges, he may not have what it takes to survive in the future.

Many women in your parents' generation thought they had a guaranteed future when they married. Luanne says, "I had my life mapped out by the time I reached high school. Carl and I were going to get married, and I'd stay home and raise children. When Carl graduated, I was still in eleventh grade, but I dropped out of school so we could get married right away. My first baby was born a year later. Then—after seven years of marriage—Carl and I split up. I have three kids, no high school diploma, and no wage-earning skills."

Today, girls who make the same choice as Luanne did may face hard times. Divorce is more common than ever before. Even if your marriage stays together, having an education is important. Many couples with children find that they need two full-time incomes to make ends meet. The choice that some women in previous generations made—to stay home and take care of the children—may not be available to you.

Since there are no guarantees, it's best to have as many options as possible. Staying in school helps keep those options open. Don't deny yourself anything that you might later wish you had.

CHAPTER 3

When Getting Through School Is Tough

Q I'm Jason, and I'm 16. My grades are lousy, and I'm flunking out of school. It's driving me nuts—it's like everyone else can get the work done, but I can't. What's the point of staying in high school? I'll never get to college. Why shouldn't I just quit now and get it over with? It would be a relief.

A Are the other kids smarter than you? Probably not—they've just learned how to meet the demands of school. That's something you need to learn, too.

You'll face many challenges in your life, and getting through high school is your first big one. Now is the time to make a decision: Are you going to give up on school, or are you going to give it your best shot?

You can probably do better in school if you go about it differently. Get some help. Go to see a sympathetic teacher; explain that you're worried about your grades. The teacher may recommend special help, such as a tutor or a different class. If you have trouble concentrating, your teacher may give you some tips to help you focus better.

If you're prepared to meet that challenge of high school—and put your mind to it—you can probably succeed. On the other hand, if you choose to give up on this challenge, you may find it that much harder to face the next one.

Teens offer many reasons for dropping out. Some have problems at home or with friends—these kinds of problems are discussed in the next chapter. Others have problems with schoolwork. They say just what Jason said: "School is too much for me." For these students, changing the way they approach schoolwork may be the key to meeting the challenge of high school.

Academic Success

In high school you're expected to do well in your academic subjects, such as English, math, history, and science. For some people, doing well in these subjects is tough. They have trouble learning the material, they can't remember anything they learn, or they freeze when it comes to taking tests. When you don't do well in your classes, it can be a real blow to your self-confidence. This is one reason that some teens leave school without graduating.

If you have trouble with your schoolwork, don't give up hope. It may just be that you need to find better ways to learn and study. If you can figure out what ways work best for you, you may find schoolwork a little easier.

Different Ways of Learning

Some students learn best when teachers present information to the class. Others absorb little that they hear, but they have a photographic memory for things they read. Some students have to write things down in order to learn them; and some learn by repetition. Which technique works best for you? If you can figure that out, you can help yourself retain more.

For example, if you know you're the kind of person who learns best by listening, you could ask your teacher for permission to bring a tape recorder to class so that you can replay the lesson later when you study. Or you could read your textbook or your class notes aloud at home.

On the other hand, if you find it easier to learn by reading, you may want to take careful notes in class and review them at home. Or you might ask your teacher to recommend some books that review or supplement the class material.

Homework and Studying

Lots of students can improve their grades simply by improving their study habits. Do you do your homework in front of the television or with the radio on? Some kids think it's OK to do their homework on the bus on the way to school or in homeroom. Others copy from classmates or from reference books. These students may finish the assignment, but they've hardly learned the material. They generally won't do well on tests.

One trick successful students use is to set up a weekly study and homework schedule. For example, Carole has an after-

Students may have trouble in school for a variety of reasons. A guidance counselor can help a student identify the area of difficulty and plan a suitable program to fit that student's needs.

school job, so her weekday schedule is to go to her job from 3:00 to 6:00, have dinner at 6:00, and do homework after dinner until 9:00. She watches television or talks with her friends from 9:00 to 10:00. By setting up a schedule, Carole makes sure she has the time to do her work.

Another good way to study is to form a study group. Get together regularly with two or three friends and discuss the material. Test and retest each other until all of you understand it. Your study group can also help you practice oral reports, solve math problems, or get over difficulties in research projects. Working with others might even make doing homework fun.

There are lots of other tips that can help you do better in school. Ask your school librarian to recommend books on study habits and test-taking techniques. You might also ask your parents or teachers for advice or suggestions.

Special Education and Special Needs

Some students do poorly in school because they have certain disadvantages. These can be based on language problems, learning difficulties, or a poor educational background.

Language Problems

English is an unfamiliar language to many teens. They may be newcomers to this country, or they may have been born to parents who speak another language at home. Some of these students, while they may be very bright, don't know enough English to follow the classwork. They may need extra training in English. Many schools with high immigrant populations offer such training.

Learning Difficulties

Just as some kids have more trouble than others throwing a baseball, some have more trouble than others reading a book or doing math. Some of these students simply need more time to learn material. Others have special learning problems.

Dyslexia, for example, is a learning problem in which the brain reverses letters and words. A student with dyslexia isn't stupid; he or she just has more trouble reading than others.

Fermin, a graphic designer for a large advertising agency in New York City, is dyslexic. He remembers, "I hated any class that required me to read more than ten pages a night. I loved art classes, though, because I didn't have to deal with words or numbers at all. The only thing that got me through English and math was knowing that I could start an art career after I graduated. I could not be at the point I am today if I hadn't finished school."

If you think you have a learning problem, you might do better in a special education class. Teachers of these classes have special training in dealing with learning problems. Also, because the classes are smaller, you can get special attention. The teacher can go as quickly or as slowly as you need to learn the material. Many kids who attend special education classes do exceptionally well in their careers, because the classes help them learn how to deal with their special problems.

Gaps in Your Education

Some students come to high school unprepared for high school work. They may have been taught poorly in elementary or middle school. They may have missed many classes because of illness or an injury. When they get into high school, they feel that they're too far behind to catch up, no matter how hard they work.

If you're one of those people, you don't have to give up. There are a number of ways you can catch up. If you ask, your teacher or guidance counselor will probably be pleased to help.

Repeating a Subject

If you do poorly in a class, you may have to repeat it. That can be hard on your self-esteem. You may feel that it confirms all your fears about being stupid. Many kids see one failure or one repeated class as reason enough to drop out.

You can turn repeating a class into a positive if you look at it as a wake-up call. If you're held back, it's because your teacher knows that you need more work in the subject. It's important not just that you graduate, but that you graduate with a certain level of skills. If you don't master those skills, you'll have even more trouble later on.

Keep in mind, too, that you may be able to make up the classwork without falling behind your classmates. Special tutorial programs or summer school classes may be available—take advantage of them.

School's a Bore

Some people who think about dropping out are good at schoolwork. They understand the material quickly and then have to wait while the rest of the class catches up. Many of these students find school impossibly boring. Some of them leave school, figuring they're not learning much there anyway.

Some of these students decide to take the General Educational Development (GED) test rather than stay in school. Passing the test enables you to get a state-issued diploma. You can read more about the GED in Chapter 7. The GED shows that although you don't have a high school diploma, you know the material that high school graduates know. Many employers and college admissions officers treat a GED as identical to a high school diploma.

But taking a test is no substitute for being in high school. Remember, high school doesn't teach just academic subjects; it teaches social and cultural skills as well. Even if you know enough to get a GED, you may not be mature enough to make it in the adult world. Before you decide to leave school, try to get all you can out of it.

If your classes are too easy for you, you're probably in the wrong classes. Find out if there is an advanced class that you can transfer into. Some schools even offer college-level classes. If you don't want to switch classes, or can't, make your present classes more challenging. Ask your teacher for special projects. When you're given an assignment, don't settle for making it only "good enough"; work to make it the best you can.

Remember, too, that your school offers challenges outside of the classroom. Get involved in student government, sports, music, drama, or other extracurricular activities. The more you do, the more you'll like school.

Many bright teens find it rewarding to tutor other students. You might want to help other kids—your age or younger—with their math or reading. Not only will this help them improve their grades, but it will also help you feel better.

Where to Get Help

No matter what's holding you back from doing well in school, there are solutions. In most cases, all you need to do is ask. Share your worries with a teacher or a counselor. There's a good chance your school provides tutors, special classes, or other help for students who need it.

Tutors

Many high schools offer peer tutoring, in which upperclass students help out younger ones. Marcy was nearly ready to drop out of school during her sophomore year. Then her algebra teacher set her up with Jefferson, a senior who got high grades in math. "Jefferson was great," Marcy said. "He sat with me and went over the equations again and again until I understood them. It was just him and me, so we could go as slowly as I wanted. He didn't make me feel stupid. Together we got through the hard parts."

Tutors can help because they work one-to-one with their students. Your tutor can slow the pace when you have trouble

One on one tutoring can often help a student to catch up with a class, or review work that may be difficult to understand.

with certain topics and skip over material you understand. Your tutor can watch you work out homework problems and catch mistakes as you make them. He or she may also be able to teach you test-taking skills, help you with memorization, and offer other hints for learning the material more easily.

If your school doesn't have student tutors or if you need more help than they can offer, you might be able to find a college student who can tutor you. In some communities, private tutoring groups are available; but these cost money.

Extra Classes

Some high schools schedule special classes before or after school for students who need extra help. In these classes, tutors or teachers help students learn difficult material or review older lessons. These programs may be just what you need if you feel that you're falling behind.

Alternative Programs

Some students don't do well in regular high schools simply because of the way subjects are taught. There are all sorts of public and private schools that teach subjects in creative and different ways. Some public "free schools," for example, keep classes informal—they may encourage more "hands on" student participation and feature less lecturing by teachers. Instead of receiving letter grades every quarter, students may meet with their teachers and parents and receive written evaluations of their work. For some students, learning this way works well.

Other public school systems have "magnet schools" that focus on special subjects or special types of students. For example, Jerome plays the violin and hopes someday to be a professional violinist. But he hated spending all his time in a school where music was a one-period-a-week subject. He switched from his local high school to a magnet school for music. Like the kids in his old school, he still learns English, math, and science, but he also receives special training in music. He loves going to school now because all his classmates and the teachers share his interest in music.

Remember, you can get through school even if it's tough—but that requires work and commitment. You can look at school as a burden, complaining that you're being forced to do things that you don't want to do. Or you can look at the positive side—school is your chance to prepare for the future. In school, you're given the chance to explore your interests and test your skills. Once you've decided to face the challenges—the assignments, the papers, and the tests—each one brings you a step closer toward the future you want to make for yourself. It's up to you.

CHAPTER 4

Personal Problems

Q My name's Chris and I'm 17. My girlfriend, Sheila, is pregnant. I can't concentrate on school. I wonder if I should leave school and start earning money for the baby. Now my grades have taken a nosedive. What should I do?

A You do have a tough problem. Being a parent is a big responsibility. Life will be difficult for a while. But dropping out of school won't solve your problems. In fact, if you leave school now, you'll probably be adding to your problems.

A baby is an important reason to stay in school—not to leave it. You and Sheila are going to need money to raise your child. At first, the baby may not need much. But in time his or her needs will increase. If you stay in school, you'll earn a lot more in the future than you will if you drop out. Things may be tight at first, but in the long run, you'll be a lot better off. That's essential if you want to give yourself, Sheila, and your baby the best possible future.

That future might seem more manageable if you develop a solid plan for it. Sit down with Sheila and an adult you trust—a parent or a counselor—and figure out what you're going to do. Come up with a plan for supporting your child over the short term and preparing for your long-term future. The plan may include working part time, going to school at night, or borrowing money from a relative or friend. Look into what's available in your community to help teen parents who are in school. Knowing what you want in the future makes you more likely to attain it.

Once you've mapped out a solid plan, you may find it easier to concentrate in school. It's amazing what making sensible choices and plans can do. Of course, you may need to adjust your plan as circumstances change. But at least you'll know what your major goals are—and one way of attaining them.

• • • • • • • • • • • •

Every teen faces challenges and troubles. There are many academic, social, and physical demands on you. You may feel that you're different, unattractive, stupid, or unpopular. With

Serious personal problems may cause you to consider dropping out of school. However, there are many people—from friends and family to professional counselors—who can help you find a solution to your problem.

low self-esteem, or feelings of insecurity about your looks or intelligence, it may be hard for you to do your best or to concentrate.

In addition to these problems, some teens have extra troubles—such as an unexpected pregnancy, abuse of drugs or alcohol, run-ins with the police, or difficulties at home. With troubles like these, it may seem almost impossible to devote enough attention to school. But there are ways you can deal with these problems and still have time for school.

Pregnancy and Parenthood

Becoming pregnant does not force a teen to leave school. Many schools actively encourage teen parents and parents-to-be to stay in school. Some schools offer parenting classes so that teens who are expecting children can learn about prenatal care and caring for newborns and toddlers. They can also learn how to meet the baby's financial, medical, and other needs.

Lack of child care is a common reason that new parents leave school. To meet that need, some high schools provide child care in the school. Others offer night classes, so that one parent can attend school during the day and the other one can attend at night.

You and Your Friends

Many kids do poorly in school because of their friends. They cut classes because their friends cut classes. They disrupt their classes because their friends encourage them. Darren remembers, "When I got into high school, I started hanging out with this bunch of guys. With them, anyone who went to class was considered a real loser. They figured they had better things to do than to listen to some teacher talk about some old war. The truth was, I actually liked school, but fitting in with the guys was more important."

If your friends pressure you to stop doing schoolwork, keep in mind that it's your life they're messing with. You need to make your own decisions. Think about the consequences of your actions. While cutting school to go to the mall might be fun, think about whether or not that will help you with your future plans.

Spending time with your friends—during school, after school, and on the weekends—is fun and important. But you must balance your social life with your schoolwork. If you stay out so late that you're too tired for school—or, worse, if you get worn out doing drugs—you don't have a good balance.

Some kids who want to study find it difficult to pay attention because their friends are being disruptive. If that's your problem, talk to your friends about it. Make it clear that you treat school seriously. If they don't change, you may want to ask your teacher to move your seat or ask your counselor to put you in another class.

Trouble at Home

Some kids have trouble at school because they have trouble at home. Every family has problems from time to time. But certain situations, such as those discussed here, can make it nearly impossible for a teenager to focus on school.

Family Breakup

If your parents are divorced, divorcing, or fighting, your home may not be the quiet refuge that you need. Arguments can make it hard to concentrate. Moving to a new school district after parents divorce—or dividing time between two parents in two houses—can make it hard for you to focus on studies.

If you can't concentrate at home, you may want to set up your own study area somewhere else. Can you study at the house of a neighbor or nearby relative? Can you study with a classmate who lives in your neighborhood? You could form a study team with him or her, working every day at your friend's house or at a room in the library or youth center. None of these suggestions will help your parents with their problems, but you'll be able to get your work done.

Some teens blame themselves for their parents' divorce. They feel guilty and think the divorce is their fault. Upset by the split, they ignore school. This response is understandable but off the mark. Teens don't cause parents to divorce; parents' problems lead them to divorce. And there isn't anything that teens can do to bring them back together.

If your parents' breakup is hard to accept, it may help to talk with a counselor. He or she can help you adjust to your new life and refocus your energy in a positive way.

Economic Problems

Many families in the 1990s are suffering from economic problems. Many parents have lost their jobs and are struggling to keep their children housed and fed. In some families, the oldest child must leave school to help around the house or to earn money. If circumstances make it impossible for you to stay in school, don't give up. There may be a way for you to finish your education while you help the family.

Find out about alternative programs or night schools leading to a high school diploma, or its equivalent. The GED is discussed in greater detail in Chapter 7. It's important to get your GED if you don't finish school. It shows employers that you have the education you need to do the job.

In the long run, you'll help the family—and yourself—a lot more if you finish your education. Don't let current financial troubles cut off your future options.

Child Abuse

Some adults have trouble handling their own problems and take out their anger on their children. Many of these abused children run away from home. But running away is not a good solution to abuse. Kids who run away usually find themselves on the streets, in danger, homeless, without money, and without a future.

If a parent—or any adult—is mistreating you, you can take action to stop it. Every community has people who help children who are abused—and the abuser, too. To find help, talk to your favorite teacher, a close relative, a neighbor, a member of the clergy, or an adult friend.

Substance Abuse

Many kids drop out of school because their use of alcohol or other drugs gets out of hand. They start drinking or using drugs at parties, then after school, and then during the school day. This is what happened to Shannon. "I started drinking when my boyfriend broke up with me," she said. "Some days, I'd cut school and drink all afternoon. Well, I started drinking more and going to school less. I tried to keep my grades up, but when I went to class, I was either drunk or hung over. I had trouble concentrating on my work. I began to fall further and further behind. By the time I got over the breakup, I'd already lost a semester. Even if I stopped drinking, there'd be no way to make up the lost time."

Shannon was about to leave school, but a talk with one of her teachers changed her mind. The teacher told her about a program for teens with substance abuse problems. The program helped her get off alcohol and get back on track with schoolwork. Shannon worked hard. She needed an extra semester to catch up on what she'd missed, but she did eventually graduate.

There are many programs like this one all around the country. If you think you have a drug or alcohol problem, talk with a counselor. Even if your school doesn't have a program, the counselor can probably direct you to one run by a local group or a hospital.

School counselors have been trained to handle all sorts of problems that confront teenagers today.

Run-ins with the Law

Theo was 15 years old and a member of the 16th Street gang. "The only reason I went to school was to meet with my gang," he said. "We'd hang around the school to see if we could rip off some of the other kids. Sure, it'd be cool to get a high school diploma—I don't plan to spend my life in a gang—but what's the point? I've been arrested four times—no one's ever gonna hire me."

Some young people join gangs because they see gang life as exciting and an easy way to make quick money. Gang members often commit serious crimes such as grand theft, drug sales, or even murder. Other teens who aren't in gangs also commit crimes, such as shoplifting. They may want something they can't afford to pay for, or they may simply want to see what they can get away with.

Eventually, people who commit crimes are caught. At the police station, they're photographed and fingerprinted. These arrests become part of a permanent criminal file. Depending on the seriousness of the crime, their age, and their criminal history, they may spend time in jail or in a juvenile detention center.

Some people, like Theo, think that having a criminal record means that their lives are ruined. Many leave school, figuring that they'll never get a job and that they're doomed to be criminals all their lives. They are wrong. Having a juvenile record or a history of gang activity will make life more difficult—but not impossible. Of course, the sooner a teen decides to stay out of trouble, the easier his or her life will be.

Crime in the School

Many teens stay out of school because of people like Theo. They're scared of being robbed or hurt by gang members, of drug dealers who hang out near the school, or of classmates who carry guns, knives, and other weapons.

Every year, teens minding their own business are killed or injured simply because they were in the wrong place at the wrong time. If there is violence in your school, you have good reason to be afraid. But try not to let it deprive you of your education.

Perhaps you have relatives in another city who would let you live with them until you finish high school. Or you could do what gang members do—rely on strength in numbers. Go to school in a group. Play it safe and stay as far away as possible from the gangs. You can also work with officials to try to improve the school. Many schools have a specially trained police officer to watch over gang activities in the school. These officers are very helpful in reducing crime and protecting kids who want nothing to do with gangs. If you're ever threatened, find the officer and ask for help.

You might feel more in control if you took steps to help get the gangs out of your school and your neighborhood. Many communities have programs working to fight gang activities. Your community may have graffiti cleanup programs, neighborhood watch programs, or neighborhood beautification programs. Community leaders may work with young kids to keep them away from gangs. They'd welcome your help.

Solving Personal Problems

Dealing with any problem is easier if you have the support of other people. Check out what's available in your school. You may be surprised at what you'll find. One program, School Based Youth Services in New Jersey, is a one-stop source for students with problems—problems with drugs, families, pregnancy, suicide, or anything else. Students can see counselors and be assured that everything they say is confidential. The counselors can help them individually or put them in touch with other students who are working on the same problems. Counselors help find doctors, parenting classes, tutors, alternative education, and mental health professionals.

The program is very popular. For most of the students, finding someone who cares about them may be the best thing about it. There may be a similar program in your school or community center.

Probably the hardest part of solving a personal problem is asking for help. But once you've overcome that first obstacle, you'll find many understanding people who are willing and able to give you the help you need.

CHAPTER 5

Work and School

Q I'm Juanita. I'm 16 and I work after school. My family really needs the money I make. I could make a lot more if I left school and started to work full-time. Isn't that a good reason to leave?

A A lot of kids are in the same situation as you—they're old enough to help with the family expenses, and they feel pressured to get a full-time job. Some are pressured by their parents. Others feel that it's unfair to still be in school when their parents are working so hard.

• • • • • • • • • • • •

The truth is that if you can hold out a little longer, you'll help your family much more in the long run. Thinking about the long run is hard, but it may be best for you and your family.

What are your future plans? Do you have dreams of being a teacher or a police officer? Do you want to work in health care? Do you want to join the army or another branch of the military service? All of these careers—and most others—require at least a high school education. Many require more schooling than that. By leaving school without graduating, you may be abandoning those dreams or putting them off for a very long time. Many teens who drop out don't realize this until years later. Then they have the difficult job of going back and finishing their education.

Most of these career-oriented jobs start at salaries of at least $14,000 a year. Even if taxes and social security take one-fourth of your pay (which they usually do), you'll be bringing home about $800 a month, or $200 a week. Plus, most of these jobs will offer additional financial benefits such as paid health insurance. Most also offer the potential for advancement and better salaries as you gain experience on the job.

On the other hand, let's say you leave school now. Jobs are hard to come by, especially for uneducated people. If you do find a job, it is most likely to be uninteresting work with low pay. Let's say you do find a full-time job, perhaps stocking shelves in a store. You'll probably start at minimum wage, so you'll make about $5 an hour—with no benefits. When taxes are taken out, you'll be bringing home just over $100 a week. Ask your parents whether it's worth it for you to give up your future plans—and more income in the long run—for that $100.

Earning money to support your family is a good and important goal, but don't be shortsighted. One more year in school and you can help your family much more. This chapter discusses some alternatives to dropping out of school. One of them might work for you.

A Part-Time Job

Many students get a part-time job while in high school. This may be a good solution for you, even if your family is struggling like Juanita's. Finding a part-time job is a good way to make extra money, gain some experience, and learn a lot about the working world.

Even if you're not yet old enough to get a job, you can earn money mowing neighbors' lawns or shoveling snow. You might want to babysit—many neighbors would love to have a responsible high school student stay with their children after school or on weekends.

What You Gain

You gain a lot more than money if you have a part-time job while you're in school. Francisco remembers, "I got a job at the local hamburger place. Three months of flipping burgers gave me a real good taste of what work is like for people who drop out of school. My manager is 36 years old and only making $6 an hour more than me. Seeing what the future could hold was enough to keep me in school."

Gerry had a somewhat different experience, but came to the same conclusion. He planned to go into show business when

With a part-time or summer job, you can earn some money and get some work experience while continuing your education.

he finished school. He got an after-school job in a television studio. "Until I got the job, I thought school was an absolute waste of time. But at my job in the studio, I needed everything I was learning in school. My social studies classes helped me understand what was going on in the news programs. I even got to speak Spanish when we did an interview program on immigrants." Using skills learned in high school in a real work situation gave Gerry a whole new outlook about the work he had done in class. Getting that job helped motivate him to bring his grades up.

Working part-time while in school may help you land a full-time job when you graduate. Holding a job and keeping up with your homework shows employers that you are dedicated, able to manage your time, and able to work under pressure. It shows that you are motivated and have experience with the business world. What better way is there to convince an employer that you can be a good worker than to show you've been a good worker?

But before you apply for that part-time job, be sure you'll be able to handle both work and school. Some students can't. You'll need time to do your homework and get enough sleep. If you take on so much work that your schoolwork suffers, you're going to burn out. Then no employer is going to be impressed. You may want to consider concentrating on your schoolwork now and looking for a summer job later.

What You Give Up

Remember that there are only so many hours in a day. If you decide to get a job, you'll have less time for extracurricular activities. For some people, participating in team sports, the school play, or clubs is the best part of school. If you get an after-school job, you may have to sacrifice some of these activities.

You may also have to sacrifice some of your social life. If you work weekends, for instance, you'll have to leave Friday night parties earlier than your friends do. Remember—making money is important, but you'll have plenty of time to make money once you finish high school. Be sure to save some time and energy for other important things while you're a teen.

Getting a Jump on Your Career

The trouble with many part-time jobs is that they don't help you prepare for your career. Most high school kids get jobs working in fast-food restaurants or stocking shelves in supermarkets. But if you know what you want to do when you get out of high school, you may be able to start learning the skills you'll need.

Vocational Education Programs

Vocational education programs are ideal for students who are planning a hands-on career such as auto mechanics, construction, or carpentry. Vocational education teaches you exactly the skills you will need for your career.

Galen knew he wanted to be an auto mechanic since he was six years old. In tenth grade, he got into his school's vocational education program. "It's a whole new world," he says. "I'm learning real skills. At school, we talk about engines and oils and things that are going to be a regular part of my life. I get hands-on experience. I'm more ready than ever to start work, but now I see how much I can learn if I stay in school another couple of years."

Work Study Programs

Many high schools permit students to participate in work-study or cooperative programs. These students stay in school while they earn money and learn a trade. In these programs, students spend half their time in school and half at a workplace. Depending on what career you have planned for yourself, your workplace might be an office, a hospital, or a construction site. In some programs, students are paid for their time on the job; in other programs, students receive school credit. During the time they spend in school, students take both traditional and work-related classes.

Learning a skill, such as carpentry, may not only keep an interested student in school but pay off later on the job.

The Pennsylvania Youth Apprenticeship Program is one such program. Jenny has been in the program for a year. Two days a week, she goes to school. The other three days, she works full-time in a metalworking factory. As an apprentice, she's treated like any other worker—she is paid for her time, and she'll be fired if she does poorly. At the same time, she is monitored closely and taught as much about factory work as possible. By the time her program is over, Jenny will have learned a useful lifetime trade.

Jenny noticed that spending time on the job made her classes become more important. She says, "At the factory, we have to do a lot of math—to measure pieces and make sure they'll fit. Trial and error isn't allowed when you're cutting steel. In social studies class, we learned about labor movements and the history of people who did exactly what I'm training to do. It was fascinating. In science, we learned about why metals expand and crack. Working at my job gave math and history and science a whole new meaning."

Alternatives for Full-Time Working Students

If you choose to—or have to—leave school to earn money, you may not have to give up your high school diploma. Perhaps there's a way that you can work full-time and still graduate. Read on.

Some schools have set up independent studies programs—learning centers that students attend for as many hours as they can each day. Study and class time can be scheduled around jobs. Students in these programs work at their own pace—some can finish their schoolwork in two years; others may take four or five.

Many of these programs permit students who have left school to participate. This is why students in these programs are often older than the average high school student.

These independent study programs are an excellent way to finish your education, but they aren't easy. No one will be standing over you, urging you to do your work. You alone will carry the responsibility to finish your education.

There are other options as well. For example, you might want to switch to night school so you can earn money during the day. Or you might want to consider taking the GED—General Educational Development test for a High School Equivalency Diploma.

Getting a job is an important part of growing up. When you work, you earn money, learn about responsibility, and gain valuable skills. But getting a job is not your only goal in life. And it may not be the right time for you to get one. While you're a teenager, your number one goal should be to get the education you need. If you choose to work while you finish school, be sure that you don't lose sight of that main goal.

Interview

Few people are better able to judge the abilities of people who've graduated from high school as compared to dropouts than employers. Employers see workers of both types day in and day out. They see their skills, their work habits, and their attitudes. They hire and supervise people of many different backgrounds.

Sandy is such an employer. She used to hire assembly-line workers to manufacture mailing machines and electronic scales. She hired people who were high school graduates, people who had dropped out of school, and people who'd gone back to earn their GEDs. She noticed quite a few differences among the three groups.

When I interviewed someone for a job, I always looked at how they related to me—did they look me in the eye when I was talking to them, or were they constantly looking down, or looking around? Another factor was how well they could interpret a question and respond.

From what I've seen, high school graduates are more mature. They tended to fit in a little better. They had a lower level of fear, if you will, or less reservation about entering into a large group of people. That's important, because on an assembly line, you could be working around hundreds of employees. We had about 300, 350, up to as many as 500 at one time. Those who had a high school education seemed to fit in a little easier; they adjusted to the environment a little quicker.

I also felt more secure hiring a high school graduate. I saw the person with a high school education as having a stick-to-it approach to life—as not being a quitter. I figured that such a person would stick to the job and not leave after two months. You see, turnover is very costly to a company. Employers spend a certain amount of time and money training new employees—telling them about the company and its policies and procedures as well as how to perform the job. That's a cost to a company. If an employee leaves shortly after being hired, that training cost is just wasted. I wanted to hire someone who wouldn't waste my time, and high school graduates seemed to be a better bet.

The communication skills a person learns in school are important, too—I don't mean written skills as much as verbal. Assemblers really didn't have to write memos or letters, but they did have to fill out forms, and they had to report failures. I think that someone with a high school education has more experience in filling out forms and reading and interpreting a set of instructions.

School provides a valuable background in math, too. There was some quick math the workers had to do. There was a meter, and we had to test it for postage. The worker had to keep track of how much postage was used. Learning math in high school made this task a lot easier—and the work more accurate.

I think that school provides you with more than an education from the standpoint of learning only facts. It is just as important to be challenged and to feel confident that you can meet the challenge and don't need to be afraid of it. Face it, you're going to meet challenges in your employment years; you're going to meet them later in your relationships with everybody you come into contact with. It's that building of self-confidence that's a real value in high school.

When I started working, I had some really tough times. I had to learn to adjust to different personalities and different ways of looking at things—it wasn't always just my way. I think high school prepares you for that. In the classroom, all the students are different—some do better than others. And the teachers are different. Some teachers are more fair than others—and that's like the real world. Some bosses aren't very fair either, and that's a fact of life, like it or not. So I think that's what you gain by staying in high school—self-confidence in the sense of refining your interpersonal skills.

So I would definitely encourage people to stay in school—there's no doubt about it. The higher the education you have in your pocket, the more resources are available to you in terms of what you want to do in your future. And employers definitely look at that.

I saw people with GEDs as people who at least had the courage to recognize they'd made a mistake and then took the time and made the effort to fix it. Usually people who go back for a GED do so because they want to. It shows that there's been a change in their lives, and if they had made mistakes earlier, they've corrected them.

What's good about the GED is that digging deep inside of you. First, you must admit that you made a wrong decision; second, you must overcome very low self-esteem. That's very hard to do. I think the person willing to do that shows some guts, and I think anyone who does it should be very proud of it. That's not to say that everybody who drops out has low self-esteem. But I think that a large number of them do. I know that if I had dropped out of high school, I would have had those feelings. And it would have taken a lot out of me personally, as an individual, as a human being, to make that decision to go back.

I'm impressed by an applicant who says, "Well, you know, I came to the realization that I'd made a mistake, and so I chose this year to go back to school while I worked at a couple of after-school side jobs mowing lawns to try to make a little extra money." That's the type of person that I really felt would be an asset to the corporation.

As far as promotion, it was how well you did—the previous station you worked on—more than whether you had a high school diploma or a GED or had not graduated. It really was based on your attendance and performance in the position that you were holding. But when workers were reaching toward the final job stations, where paperwork became involved, the situation was different. All else being equal, if you had two people working, coming up through the ranks, both performing well in their previous stations, both having good attendance, neither having problems with management, and one had an education and one didn't, I'd bet you anything that the person with the education would get the advancement.

Without a college degree, of course, professional and management positions are closed. Probably less than 3 percent of these openings went to someone who had no education. Usually the workers were stopped by their communications skills. When you start getting up into those semiprofessional and management-type positions, you need to be good at communication—you need writing skills and oral skills and analytical skills. When you're coming up in an assembly line, you don't need those skills. So if you didn't learn them in school, and you haven't had a job where you had the opportunity to learn them and use them, then you probably don't have them now. You may be a little more refined, simply because you're mature—you've got a few more years' experience and you've been in the world a little longer—but you don't really have that level of skill that you need in order to move up into those higher positions. So I would say that except in extremely rare situations, it would be very, very, very difficult for a person without an education—be it a high school diploma, or college courses, or something of that nature—to move into upper-level positions in a company.

The starting position pays about $12,000. That's entry-level—someone with no experience, just coming in. With experience, that might go up to $16,000 or $18,000. So if you had an individual without an education, who was an average or below-average performer at the station—someone who wasn't promoted to the higher station levels—that worker would probably make up to $16,000 to $18,000 before being what we call "capped out." Then that worker couldn't really earn any more, no matter how long he or she stayed with the company.

CHAPTER 6

The Business World

Q My name is Terri and I'm 16. I absolutely hate school. It's boring and a waste of time. Sure, I've heard that working is a pain—but if I left school and got a job, at least I could make some money. Doesn't that make sense?

A You're right that work can often be a pain, especially if you're not prepared for it. Many kids make the mistake of leaving school for the wrong reasons. Some leave because they think school restricts their freedom too much. Then they get a job and find they have less freedom than they ever had in school. Others leave school because they think "the real world" is glamorous. Then they discover that the jobs they can get are pretty dull.

You know what you'll be leaving behind if you drop out of school. The question is, do you know what's ahead? When you have a job, you have a boss. The boss tells you what to do, watches you, and has authority over you. The boss tells you when to be at work, what you can wear, and when you can leave. The boss tells you when you may take lunch, and for how long. You'll have a day off here and there, but you'll no longer have a week off for Christmas or a summer vacation. You'll definitely have more rules to follow than you did in school.

Keep in mind, too, that the newest employees usually get the least desirable work. For example, if you took a job at the local 24-hour store, you might get the shift that starts at 6:00 a.m. You'd have to get up earlier than you ever did as a student. Or you might get the late night shift. Either way, you won't be able to go to the movies or parties with your friends who are still in school.

To find out what work is like for people who leave high school early, go talk to some of them. Ask them to describe what's best and what's worst about working. Think about whether that's the life you want.

Someday, of course, you'll have to get a job. But if you wait until you finish school, you'll be able to get a better job—with higher pay and more respect. Leaving school because "it's a bore" is a mistake. Wouldn't it be awful to leave school and get stuck at someplace even more boring?

The Job Market

There aren't a lot of jobs out there for people without high school diplomas—and every year, there are even fewer. In today's economy, there are many more unemployed people than there are jobs. Employers can be selective and require certain minimum qualifications—such as a high school diploma. If you don't meet those qualifications, they won't even consider interviewing you for a position. Whether or not you think a diploma is important doesn't matter to most employers. They think it's important.

The jobs available for high school dropouts tend to be dead-end jobs with very little room for advancement. Many dropouts end up doing restaurant work—waiting tables, cleaning tables, cleaning dishes—or custodial or janitorial work. Others find work as machine operators or maintenance and repair people. Some get hired as laborers—for farmers, ranchers, house builders, carpenters, or electricians—and others find work as truck drivers or security guards.

Most entry-level jobs pay low wages, have few benefits, and offer little room for advancement.

One problem with many of these jobs (besides low pay and few benefits) is that they tend to be unstable. These are the jobs that are often eliminated during the off-season or when times are bad. Housing construction, for example, is affected greatly by seasonal and economic changes. So even if you get a job, helping a builder, you cannot be sure how long you'll have it.

Earning a Living

Many entry-level jobs pay very little. If you leave school and get a job, will you be able to live on what you earn? Will your parents continue to feed you, house you, and buy you clothes? If so, that's great, but for how long will they do that? At some point, you'll have to move out on your own.

Before you take the plunge and leave school, do some research and a little bit of math. Come up with a budget. How much will you need to spend on food? What will your rent be? How much will you spend on car expenses, clothes, and utility bills? You'll want to have some money to go to the movies or to concerts. You'll want some savings, too, right? And some money for emergencies.

How much money will you need to meet all the items on your budget? How much can you make? Nearly one-fourth of your paycheck will be taken out in taxes, so be sure to subtract that amount. Work it out—will you really be able to support yourself?

Planning a Career

Even if you find a job that can support you, you probably won't want to keep that job forever. At some point, you'll want to find a more satisfying job—a job that might lead to a real career.

For most people, a satisfying job is one that pays enough to live on, is interesting, requires some skills, and makes you feel useful. Have you given much thought to what sort of job would be right for you?

Are you artistic? Do you like a physically active job? Would you rather work outdoors or spend your days at a computer? Do you like working with people? Do you like working with your hands?

What have you done that you've been really proud of? What are your hobbies? Could any of the skills you've learned from your hobbies be used in a job? For example, Max loved to build things. Since he was a little child, he was always building birdhouses with his dad and making birthday presents for his parents and friends. He would spend hours at home in the garage designing and building more elaborate creations. When he left school, he got a job as a carpenter's apprentice, and now he's a carpenter himself, building and renovating houses.

Explore Your Options

If you're like Max and you know what you want to do; that's terrific. If not, do some investigation and explore your options. Your school counselor may be able to give you career aptitude tests or a career interest inventory. In career aptitude tests, you answer questions about what you like and don't like about school, what sort of workplace you'd like, and what talents you have. These can help you pick a career that suits you.

For example, when Tran took an aptitude test, he said his favorite subject is science. He said he hates sitting at a desk all day and he loves working with people. His school counselor suggested that he might like a job as an environmentalist and guide with the National Park Service, a job that he'd never considered before.

As you explore, don't exclude things you haven't tried—there are careers out there that you've probably never heard of. And be flexible. As you explore, you may find that the jobs you want require more schooling than you have. As a result, you may want to reconsider your plans to leave school. But that's what being in school is all about—learning about life. It's certainly not too late to change your plans. The more flexible you are now, the more options you'll have in the future.

The Job Search

Finding a job won't be easy. If you look in the newspaper, you may see hundreds of jobs advertised. The truth is that dozens of people apply for each of the jobs listed. When you answer "help wanted" ads, your competition is likely to be fierce. When a new hotel opened in Chicago a few years ago, thousands of people applied for the 300 new positions that were being offered.

Common sense should tell you not to leave school until you have someplace to go. Only half the people who drop out of high school are able to find full-time employment. The rest struggle with poverty, boredom, and difficult times.

Jayne's plan was to be a photographer. She left high school six months before graduation, hoping to start her career by getting a job as a photographer's assistant. Jayne remembers, "At first, I only answered ads for photo assistants. After three months of rejections, I got more desperate. I applied for jobs at one-hour photo shops. No one would hire me—they all told me that they had more applicants than they could ever use. I began applying for anything. I ended up getting three part-time jobs, none of which were in photography. I was so tired by the end of the day that I didn't have time to look for photo work." After a year working in a factory, waiting tables, and working as a store clerk, Jayne went back to school.

Do yourself a great favor and don't leave school until you're employed.

On-the-Job Training

The best kinds of jobs offer on-the-job training. On-the-job training gives you the opportunity to earn money while you learn important skills. If you're interested in hands-on work, such as manufacturing or construction, on-the-job training may be ideal. Talk with your school counselor about what's available.

Keep in mind that more and more on-the-job training programs exclude high school dropouts. So before you leave school, investigate whether any such programs would be open to you.

Annual Earnings by Occupation and Level of Education, 1987

Occupation	Less than High School	High School	4 Years College or More
Managerial occupations	$22,306	$23,286	$37,252
Technicians & related support occupations	$16,207	$21,358	$28,004
Marketing & sales occupations	$13,746	$17,654	$32,747
Administrative support (incl. clerical)	$15,535	$16,554	$20,823
Service occupations	$10,764	$13,093	$21,381
Repair occupations	$20,465	$25,140	$30,938
Laborers	$15,365	$19,303	$22,114
Agriculture, forestry, fishing	$10,571	$12,730	$17,130

Source: U.S. Bureau of Labor Statistics.

Highly skilled jobs have greater educational requirements. However, they also offer greater rewards, such as higher salaries and more opportunities for advancement.

On the Job

When you do get a job, be prepared to work hard. For many people, keeping a job can be harder than finding one. Remember, jobs aren't like school—you can be fired if you're often absent or late. You can be fired if you don't get along with your boss or if you don't follow the rules. Bosses are often especially hard on the newest employees, so be prepared for some stressful weeks when you first begin a new position.

Changing Your Mind

No decision is forever. If you leave school and then find that you want to go back, you can. You may be able to return to your high school. Or you may be able to get your GED. Or you may be able to find an adult education program that will give you the education you need.

We all change our minds about things. There's nothing wrong with that. The important thing is not to get hung up on living with a past decision if you feel it's no longer the right one. Maybe you see your past decision as a mistake now. That's fine; you can fix it. It's an even bigger mistake to not change.

CHAPTER 7

Getting Back on Track

Q I'm Carl and I'm 19 years old. I left school three years ago because I hated it. I've had a few jobs since then, but they've all gone nowhere. I'm beginning to think that quitting school was the wrong thing to do. Is it too late for me to go back? Is there anything I can do to get my life back on track?

A Is it too late? Absolutely not! At age 19, you may still be young enough to return to your old high school. Or, more likely, you may want to enroll in a special program for adult high school students. Many public schools and community colleges have developed programs especially for people like you, who want a second chance. To find out about what's available, start by calling your local high school. Someone there can tell you your options and explain how you can get started.

Keep in mind that school may not be any more interesting now than it was three years ago. You'll be facing many of the same challenges that you faced before. You'll have homework, you'll be given tests, and you'll have to study hard. But you're older now, and your three years of work experience may have changed your attitude about things. You may even find you actually like these academic challenges this time around.

It takes courage and hard work to go back to school. You've shown an important sign of maturity just by asking about your options. You should be proud of yourself for taking this very important step.

Why Go Back?

Lots of kids leave school, and for lots of reasons. Some of them do well in life without ever finishing their education. But those who do are rare. Most people who drop out of school regret their decision. They decide they want to go back to school.

Times Are Hard

The most common reason most people decide to go back to school is economic. Life is difficult for people without diplomas. Less than half of the people who leave school are able to find full-time employment. The others are lucky if they can find temporary or part-time jobs.

Those who find work are often unhappy with the work they find. The jobs they get offer no challenge and little chance for advancement. Of course, a high school diploma isn't any guarantee of employment. But many people are finding that not having a diploma guarantees an unending struggle to make ends meet.

Things Change

Candy was an attractive teenager. She did some modeling when she was 13 and decided she wanted to do it professionally. She remembers, "Everyone told me the younger you start the better. So I left school when I was 15 and moved to New York City. I did some modeling for teen magazines. As I got older, less work came in. By the time I was 17, I was told I was too old for teen magazines. There were hundreds of women my age competing for all the adult modeling jobs. There I was—17 years old, away from home, with no income, and nothing but a tenth-grade education." Candy decided to go back to school.

Many young people find that their ideas about school change as they grow older. Lots of things that made sense to a person 15 years old may no longer make sense at 19 or 20. Fortunately, all of us are free to change our minds as Candy did. We can all change the direction our lives are taking.

Going Back to High School

If you are young enough, your old high school may let you pick up where you left off. You'll be a little older than your classmates, but you'll be able to take advantage of all that the school has to offer. You'll have the benefit of structured, regular assignments, and feedback from teachers. You'll be surrounded by students who are learning at the same pace you are—students you can turn to for help. And perhaps most important,

It's never too late to return to school. Most communities offer alternative high school programs for adults.

you'll be able to take part in extracurricular activities. Many students find that their participation in the school play or newspaper is the most important part of their high school experience.

Alternative Programs

Many dropouts are too old to go back to a regular high school. Fortunately, these people have another option: alternative high school programs for adults. Many cities and towns offer these programs. Because of their special approach, these programs have helped tens of thousands of adults who missed out on their high school education.

Frequently these programs offer independent study. Students are encouraged to come to school whenever they can and as much as they can. A typical program is open from early in the morning to late in the evening. Students can come for one hour or several hours, one day a week or every day. (Of course, the more time they devote to classes, the sooner they graduate.) Some programs even allow students to take courses by mail, so they can get a diploma even if they live far from the school.

The adult high school program was ideal for Larisa: "I was unemployed and had a lot of catching up to do. I wanted to get my high school diploma as quickly as possible." She went to class every day, for six hours a day, and graduated in a year. The program also worked for Kim Ha. He says, "I had a full-time job. I wasn't making a lot of money at the job, but I had a baby to support. I really wanted to go back to school, but I couldn't stop working altogether." Kim Ha went to school two nights a week, for three hours each night. It took him over two years to graduate, but now he has his diploma and can get a better job.

In addition to a flexible schedule and individualized support, many of these programs offer vocational training. They also offer job-seeking skills, such as how to put together a resumé and how to do well in interviews.

Most of the students in these programs are adults, and quite a few are in their 20s and 30s. The advantage of this is that you don't have to worry about feeling out of place or being too old to attend. The disadvantage is that you're treated as an adult rather than as a high school student. The responsibility for doing the work is yours alone—no one will be there to look over your shoulder. Teachers and counselors will give you as much help and attention as you need, but the burden is on you to learn the material. If you don't do the work, you don't get your diploma.

To find out if there are such programs in your area, call the local high school. If no one there can answer your questions, check with the nearest community college or adult education program. You may be surprised to find that there are people right around the corner who are ready to help you.

The High School Equivalency Diploma

Some people leave school just before graduation. They have as much education as those who do graduate; all they lack is a diploma. These people are often blocked from certain jobs because they don't have "that piece of paper" that proves how much they know.

For these individuals, every state offers a high school equivalency diploma. It's called a General Educational Development test, or GED. To get your GED, you have to pass a two-day test. The test measures your spelling, grammar, reading, math, and writing abilities. It also tests your knowledge of social studies, natural sciences, and literature. GED eligibility varies from state to state. To obtain accurate information, you should contact the Department of Education in your county or state.

There are a number of books that can help you prepare for the GED test. These books offer detailed reviews of the subjects

What You Should Know About the GED Test

What Is the GED Test?

The initials GED stand for General Educational Development. The GED test is also referred to as the High School Equivalency Test. The GED test gives you a chance to earn a certificate that is the *equivalent* of a high school diploma. You do not have to go back to school to get it. The GED test was created in 1942 during World War II to allow veterans to get a certificate quickly that would be equivalent to a high school diploma so that they could go on to college. Later the test was made available to all adults.

Why Take the Test?

Every state in the United States, the District of Columbia, and many Canadian provinces use GED test results as the basis for giving high school equivalency credentials. Many colleges and universities now accept satisfactory GED test scores in place of completed high school grade transcripts for admissions purposes. Some labor unions even require their members who do not have high school diplomas to take the GED test.

How Much Does It Cost to Take the Test?

In many states there is no fee at all for taking the GED test. States that do require a fee charge between two and ten dollars. Check with a local high school or test center to find out if there is a fee in your area.

Where Is the Test Given?

The GED test is given at more than 3,000 official testing centers in the United States and Canada. Check with a local high school to find out the center nearest you.

Who Takes the Test?

Each year, more than half a million people take the GED test. All adult citizens of the United States are eligible to take the GED test, provided they meet the age and residency requirements for their own state, territory, or district. If you are interested in knowing if there are any special requirements for your area, you should call an adult education center or the office of the superintendent of schools in your district for more information.

What Is the GED Test Like?

Most questions on the GED test are multiple choice, and there are five answers for each question. You will need to mark one of the five answer spaces for each question. You will also have to write a short essay for the writing skills test.

Most employers and college admissions officers consider the GED to be as good as a high school diploma.

you'll be tested on. They include practice tests so you can see which areas you need help in. Many also offer general tips for improving your performance on the tests.

Though some people are able to prepare for the GED on their own, others need extra help. For those people, most public high schools, adult education programs, and community colleges also offer GED classes. Some GED candidates find it useful to hire a private tutor to help them prepare for the test.

The GED is a difficult test, but don't worry if you don't pass it the first time. You can take it as many times as you need until you pass. In the end, it will be worth all the effort. Your GED is your "piece of paper"—your proof that you have the same knowledge as any high school graduate. Most employers consider a GED to be just as good as a high school diploma.

Getting Ahead by Going Back

The idea of going back to school may seem frightening, but it shouldn't. You know you're not too stupid to do the work. Chances are you could have graduated if you had put your mind to it.

When you left school, you weren't motivated to work for a diploma. But things are different now—you've seen what life is like for people who don't have a high school education. Now you have the motivation to complete what you didn't complete before. That motivation—and the willingness to do some hard work—is all you need.

As you struggle with homework and study for your tests, keep the future in mind. Once you have your diploma or GED, you'll be much better able to find and keep a job that will meet your needs. You'll also have the self-respect that comes from facing and meeting a challenge. That self-respect is one of the most important things you'll earn in your lifetime.

Where to Go for Help

Several national organizations that can help you learn more about staying in school and planning your career are listed below. However, for the most accurate information you should contact local organizations. To find these groups, talk to your school counselor or a teacher or look in your telephone book for agencies sponsored by your city or county or by a local religious, civic, or youth organization.

National Organizations

Boys and Girls Clubs of America
771 First Avenue
New York, NY 10017
(212) 351-5900

The Fifth Ward Enrichment Program
4014 Market Street, Suite 105
Houston, TX 77020
(713) 229-8353

Summer Training and Education Program (STEP)
399 Market Street
Philadelphia, PA 19106
(215) 592-9099

Teenage Pregnancy and Parenting Project (TAPP)
1325 Florida Avenue
San Francisco, CA 94110
(415) 695-8300

The Youth Action Program
YouthBuild Coalition
366 Marsh Street
Belmont, MA 02178
(617) 489-3400

Hot Lines

A Call for Help (Canada)
(800) 537-2229

National Runaway Switchboard
(800) 621-4000

The Nineline
(800) 999-9999

Youth Crisis Hot Line
(800) 448-4663

Youth Services Bureau (Canada)
(612) 729-1000

For More Information

Books

Complete GED Preparation. Steck-Vaughn, 1991.

GED Program: Comprehensive Book. Cambridge Adult Education, 1993.

Johnson, Eric W. *How to Live with Parents and Teachers.* Westminster, 1986.

Keltner, Nancy. *If You Print This, Please Don't Use My Name.* Terra Nova Press, 1992.

Landau, Elaine. *Teenagers Talk about School.* Julian Messner, 1988.

Lang, Denise V. *But Everyone Else Looks So Sure of Themselves.* Shoe Tree Press, 1991.

Mayer, Barbara. *How to Succeed in High School.* NTC Publishing, 1992.

Passing the GED. Glencoe, 1993.

Steck-Vaughn GED (a series of GED preparation books including Writing Skills, Writing Sample, Science, Social Studies, Mathematics, and Reading). Steck-Vaughn, 1991.

Vedral, Joyce L. *I Can't Take It Anymore.* Ballantine, 1987.

Wirth, Claudine G., and Mary Bowman-Kruhm. *I Hate School: How to Hang In and When to Drop Out.* Thomas Y. Crowell, 1986.

Videotapes

"Dropout Prevention: Nowhere to Go," United Learning, 1991.

"Lean on Me," 1989.

INDEX